HOCUS POCUS
HOTEL

Hocus Pocus Hotel is published by Stone Arch Books
A Capstone Imprint
1710 Roe Crest Dr.
North Mankato, Minnesota 56003
www.capstonepub.com

Designed by Kay Fraser
Photo credits: Shutterstock

Library of Congress Cataloging-in-Publication Data
Dahl, Michael.
Out the rear window / by Michael Dahl ; illustrated by Lisa Weber.
p. cm. -- (Hocus pocus hotel)
Summary: When Charlie Hitchcock, the smartest kid at school, gets a note from the school bully, Tyler Yu, demanding a meeting he fears the worst--but it turns out that Tyler wants him to solve the mystery of the missing magician at the Abracadabra Hotel.
ISBN 978-1-4342-4038-5 (library binding)
1. Magicians--Juvenile fiction. 2. Magic tricks--Juvenile fiction. 3. Hotels--Juvenile fiction. [1. Mystery and detective stories. 2. Magic tricks--Fiction. 3. Hotels, motels, etc.--Fiction.] I. Weber, Lisa K., ill. II. Title.
PZ7.D15134Out 2012
813.6--dc23   2012000330

Printed in the United States of America
in North Mankato, Minnestoa.
042012   006682CGF12

Out the Rear Window

BY MICHAEL DAHL

ILLUSTRATED BY LISA K. WEBER

STONE ARCH BOOKS™
a capstone imprint

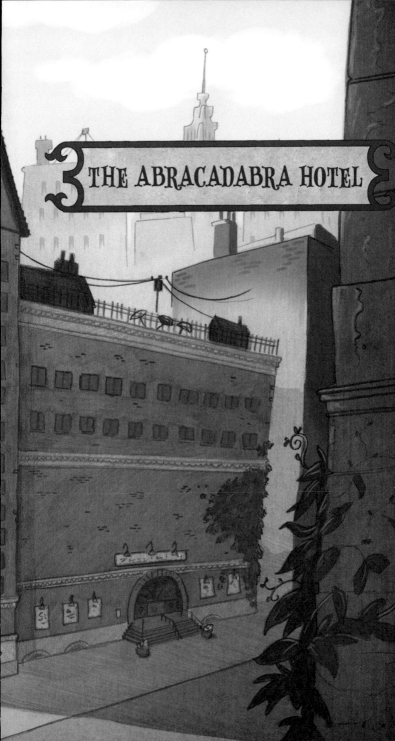

3 THE ABRACADABRA HOTEL

Table of

Contents

The Not-So-Secret Meeting

Charlie Hitchcock needed a big, angry dog.

He needed a bodyguard.

He needed guts.

But, unluckily, Charlie didn't have any of those things.

Which is why he walked out of school at the end of the day to face his fate alone. Well, not exactly alone. Kids were lined up on both sides of the sidewalk, staring at him as he walked past.

"Good luck, Charlie."

"It'll be over soon."

"You're doomed, loser."

There were friends and well-wishers. There were kids who'd never heard of Charlie until that day, the kind of kids who went to car races hoping to see a crash. And there were enemies.

A few of them shook his hand. One girl cried. A third-grader asked Charlie for his autograph.

"Maybe it'll be worth something," the young kid explained. "After, you know, you're destroyed."

After more shouts of support, nervous whispers, laughs, and jeers, Charlie reached the end of the sidewalk. He sighed. Before he walked across the street, where he would be officially off school grounds, he turned around. The crowd had split apart, as his audience left the school grounds, moving away from him as quickly as they could.

Charlie shivered in the cold October breeze. He dug deep into his pocket and pulled out the piece of wrinkled notepaper he had been handed earlier in the day, between English and American History. For the thirty-seventh time, he read it.

MEET ME AFTER SCHOOL AT 1313
GIDEON STREET. ALLEY IN BACK.
DON'T SHOW THIS TO ANYONE!!!!

The paper had been shoved into his hand by the biggest seventh-grader at Blackstone Middle School, Tyler Yu.

Ty had never spoken to Charlie in the six years they had known each other. Ty never spoke to anyone. Charlie had heard him yell, though, and grunt and shout. Because the one thing Tyler Yu was famous for was fighting. His muscles and his temper were always getting him into trouble. After-school battles between Ty and other students were legendary. And they always started with a note.

So why had Ty picked on Charlie this time? And why had he given him an address for somewhere in the middle of the city? Ty's fights usually took place in the woods behind the school.

Charlie knew he should have gone home and hidden under his bed.

That's what his best friend Andrew told him to do when Charlie showed him the note during American History. But Charlie hadn't gone home.

Charlie couldn't help it. He may not have felt brave, but he wanted to see this thing through to the end.

The one thing that always drove Charlie nuts was not knowing the answer to a puzzle or riddle or secret. Charlie was curious, and Ty's note was a puzzle. He had to know what it meant.

Thirty minutes of walking the busy sidewalks of Blackstone brought Charlie to the alley behind Gideon Street. A blue neon sign shined near the entrance. The sign was in the shape of a top hat with a blue neon rabbit peeking out of it.

"Hey!" an unfamiliar voice muttered.

Charlie made out a tall shadow in the middle of the alley. It was Ty, standing next to a big metal garbage bin.

So that's why he told me to come here, Charlie thought. *So he could throw me in with the rest of the trash.*

Ty was wearing jeans, a T-shirt, his chain-wallet, and a pair of scuffed work boots. That was what he always wore. Along with a sour expression.

He looks angry, thought Charlie. And Ty did. Even his spiky black hair looked angry.

Suddenly, Ty tossed open the lid of the garbage bin. The heavy lid swung back and struck the side of the brick building with a loud bang. "Hurry up, Hitch!" ordered Ty.

Charlie walked closer. *At least the garbage is in plastic bags,* he thought. *Maybe it won't smell so bad.*

"I said, hurry up!" Ty said. He lifted a giant bag of garbage from the ground with one hand, as if it weighed no more than a kitten. Without taking his eyes off Charlie, he slung the garbage into the bin and slammed the lid shut. Then Ty walked over to a door in the side of the brick building. He yanked it open and barked, "Inside."

Charlie did what he was told. The metal door slammed behind him.

He was alone in a dark room with Tyler Yu. This was it. The end. In the dim light that leaked under another door, Charlie saw Tyler raise his fist.

Charlie wanted to close his eyes, but he didn't. He kept them open and braced himself for the punch. "What do you want?" he whispered. Then he saw a finger poke out of Ty's fist.

"You," said Ty. "I need your help."

Abracadabra

Ty pushed Charlie toward another door. He opened it, and then shoved the smaller boy into a large open space.

"Wow!" said Charlie. They were standing at the side of a room as big as their school's gym.

Tall marble pillars held up a distant ceiling of gold-painted shapes. A blood-red carpet covered the wide floor. Palm trees grew in giant pots, and enormous chairs and couches lurked in shadowy corners.

"It's just a hotel," said Ty.

"It's not just a hotel," Charlie said. "It's the Hocus Pocus Hotel. I've heard of this place."

"First of all, that's not its name," Ty said, his face darkening. "Secondly, it's where I live, okay? My mom's the manager of the hotel and my dad's the chef. He's not a cook, he's a chef, got it?"

Charlie raised his hands. "I got it."

"We live over there, way back behind the counter." Ty pointed to a wide marble counter, where two guests were checking in to the hotel.

The rest of the lobby was empty, although Charlie thought he saw a few shadows moving among the massive pieces of furniture.

Then he saw the painting.

The man in the painting wore a skinny black tuxedo and held a top hat in his left hand.

He looked young, with thick black hair, dark eyes, and a thin black mustache that ended in two spirals. Behind the man was a woman with golden hair, lying inside a box, being sawed in half.

The painting hung near the entrance of the hotel. It was the first thing visitors saw as they walked through the front doors. And Charlie couldn't take his eyes off of it. There was something about it that he really liked. It seemed mysterious.

"Who's that?" asked Charlie, stepping closer for a better look.

"That's the guy who built this place," said Ty. "He's a magician. I mean, *was* a magician. He built this place, like, a hundred years ago. He made it for other magicians to live in once they retired. But now other people stay here, too, like when they're on vacation or whatever."

"Magicians, huh?" said Charlie. That explained the blue neon sign by the alley, with the top hat and the rabbit. "Why does it say Abracadabra under this guy's portrait?"

"That's his name. The name of the hotel, too," said Ty. "The Abracadabra. Like I said."

Charlie shoved his hands into his pockets. He felt the folded piece of notepaper, and remembered why he was standing there in the first place. "So, what do you want me to do?" he asked.

Ty frowned. He grabbed Charlie by his shirt and pulled him behind a pillar. They were hidden by palm branches and giant vases. Ty made a fist again. "Don't tell anyone about this," he ordered, "or this fist goes right through your face and out the other side."

"Tell what?" asked Charlie. "About the Abracadabra guy?"

Ty shook his head in disgust. He reached around for the chain-wallet in his back pocket and opened it. He pulled out a folded piece of paper — a picture torn from a magazine — and held it up to Charlie's nose. "See this?" Ty said.

"Uh, it's a dirt bike," said Charlie.

"Not just any dirt bike," said Tyler. "It's a Tezuki Slamhammer 750, Edition 6, in cherry-pop lightning red. And it's mine. Almost. I got money saved up from working here at the hotel."

Ty stood back and gazed at the picture. "I'm getting it as soon as school's out." He paused. "But not if you can't fix this problem."

"What problem?" said Charlie.

Ty carefully folded the paper and tucked it away. He stared hard at Charlie and said, "One of the magicians has disappeared."

Now You See Him, Now You Don't

"Disappeared?" Charlie repeated.

"One of the old guys wasn't paying his bills," said Ty. "He's been staying here for years, but all of a sudden he stopped paying his rent. He's one of the retired magicians. Mr. Madagascar."

Ty looked around quickly, as if he were afraid someone might be listening. Then he motioned for Charlie to follow him past the potted palms and into an even darker corner. They sat down behind a painted screen covered with dragons.

"I have a lot of jobs around here," Ty explained. "One of them is to pick up their rent once a month. If someone's late, I go talk to them and see if they're having a problem."

You probably scare them, too, thought Charlie.

Ty was tall and muscular, and not someone to mess with or lie to.

"So I was supposed to go up and talk to Mr. Madagascar a few days ago," Ty went on. "But I didn't."

"Why not?" Charlie asked.

"I was in the middle of an epic battle in *Empire of Blood*, okay?" Ty said.

That was the first thing Ty had said that really made sense to Charlie. Charlie spent a lot of time after school on his own favorite game, *Sherlock Holmes Maximum Z*, a detective mystery adventure. He understood how important it was to concentrate on a battle or investigation.

"I was slaughtering everyone," Ty said with a grin. "No one could beat me. There was no way I was stopping. In a few hours I finished the battle, and when it was done, I forgot about Mr. M. I didn't remember until the next day at school. So I rushed home and ran up to Mr. M.'s room, but he was gone."

"Maybe he'll come back," said Charlie. "Maybe he went on a trip."

"I don't think so," said Ty. "Come on, I'll show you his apartment."

Charlie followed Ty back into the main lobby. As they walked past the counter, the girl with the pigtails waved at Ty and said hello. Ty grumbled something and kept walking. The girl just smiled.

"Who's that?" asked Charlie. "Your sister?"

Ty made a face. "Her name's Annie Solo. She works here in the afternoons," he said. "And I don't have a sister. I'm an only child. Thank goodness."

They stopped in front of a row of three elevators. The doors looked like they were carved from gold. Above each door, a gold half-circle with a golden arrow indicated what floor the elevator was on.

A bell rang and the elevator doors on the far left slid open.

"Our luck," said Ty. "It's Brack's elevator."

The elevator was lined in faded red leather. To one side stood a thin, elderly man in a maroon-and-black uniform. He smiled a wrinkly smile as he saw Ty.

"Good afternoon, Master Yu," he said in a deep, clear voice. "A friend of yours?"

"This kid?" said Ty, nodding toward Charlie. "Nope. That's just Hitch."

"Short for Hitchcock," said Charlie. "Charlie Hitchcock is my name."

"Ah, like the famous director, Alfred Hitchcock," said the operator. "*Rear Window, Psycho, The Birds.*"

"What are you talking about?" asked Tyler. "What birds?"

"Hitchcock directed some of the world's greatest films, like *The Birds*," replied Brack. "He was the master of suspense."

"Yeah?" Tyler said. "Well, *this* Hitchcock is just here doing a report for school about the hotel. I was telling him about the magicians and stuff. You know, that kind of thing."

The older man nodded slowly. "Ah, yes. One must beware the great Abracadabra," he said. "There is magic in its walls."

Ty chuckled and glanced over at Charlie. "Brack's always saying things like that," Ty said.

"It is true, Master Yu," said the elevator operator. "Things happen here without explanation. Like the blackouts, for example."

"Blackouts?" Charlie repeated nervously. The last thing he needed was to get stuck in an elevator with these two weirdoes if the electricity went out or something.

"It's nothing," said Ty. "Just a little problem with the lights. They went out a few times last week. But they're fixed now."

"Um, okay," Charlie said.

"That's not the kind of magic I meant, Brack," Ty said. "I mean, you know, the magical kind. Not the electrical kind."

Brack nodded. "Master Yu will tell you. This hotel was built by magic," he said. "Never trust what you see here. Or what you don't see. People may even seem to disappear from time to time . . . but remember, it's a big hotel."

Charlie wondered if the old man was referring to Mr. Madagascar.

A strange look came over the operator's face. "Now you see him, now you don't," he said, and pointed past them toward the lobby.

Ty and Charlie both turned to look, but the lobby was empty. When they turned around, the elevator was empty, too. Brack had vanished.

Magic and Mirrors

"That's impossible," said Charlie.

"No, it's magic," said Ty. "It's the hotel."

The two boys stared at the elevator's interior. All Charlie saw was the faded red leather lining the walls.

The operator had vanished. But something about the walls didn't look right to Charlie.

"He didn't run away," said Charlie.

"Run away?" said Ty. "Brack?" He laughed. "He's too old."

A quiet chuckle echoed from within the elevator car. Goosebumps ran up and down Charlie's arms. "That's him," whispered Charlie. "That's him, laughing at us."

"It can't be," said Ty. "He's not there."

Then they heard Brack's voice loud and clear. "Perhaps I'm standing behind you."

The two boys turned again. The huge lobby seemed to have grown more shadows, but no one was standing there. Annie was still over behind the counter, talking on the phone.

When Charlie and Ty turned back to the elevator, Brack was there, smiling. "I told you," he said. "Never trust what you see here."

"Stupid magic," grumbled Ty.

Charlie's face lit up. "It's mirrors!" he exclaimed.

"What are you talking about?" said Ty.

Charlie hurried into the elevator car. "See this stain?" He pointed to a small stain on the back wall. It was about six feet from the floor. "It probably comes from people leaning against the wall," Charlie said. "The stuff in their hair rubs against the leather."

Brack's eyebrows rose up and his smile grew wider.

"But when Mr. Brack disappeared," Charlie continued, "this stain wasn't here."

"You sure?" asked Ty.

"Positive," said Charlie. He blushed and added, "My teachers say I have something called an acute visual memory. That means I remember everything I see."

"I know what it means," said Ty. "I'm not stupid. And I know about your photographic memory. Why do you think I picked you to help me?"

"I didn't say you were stupid," said Charlie. In fact, he figured someone who won epic battles in *Empire of Blood* was probably pretty smart. "I just mean that when Mr. Brack was gone, I didn't see the stain. And that means something was in front of the stain, hiding it."

"But we just saw the walls," said Ty.

"Right," said Charlie. "But not the back wall. We were actually seeing the side walls. Reflected on mirrors. It's an old magician's trick. Uh, no offense, Mr. Brack."

Brack applauded. "No offense taken," he said, smiling down at Charlie. "Excellent reasoning, young man. Now, let me show you the actual trick, since you figured out how it was done."

The operator reached out toward the walls on either side. There was a loud click. The two walls moved, swinging inward.

"See?" said Charlie. "There are mirrors on the outside of those fake walls."

Brack pulled the fronts of the fake walls together, forming a small angle inside the elevator. He was now hidden behind them, standing inside the angle.

The mirrors reflected more leather lining that had been hidden behind the fake walls. So all that the boys saw, when standing outside the elevator, were just red leather walls.

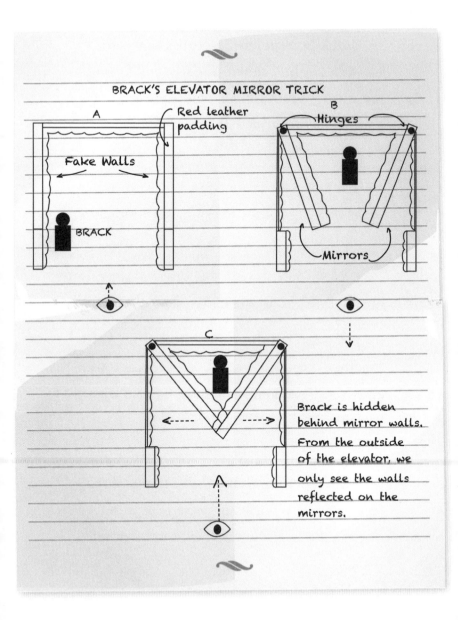

They thought they were seeing the back wall, but they were actually looking at a reflection of the two side walls. Anyone standing inside the secret angle formed by the mirrors was now invisible.

"Wow!" said Ty.

Another click, and the two mirrors moved apart. Brack stuck his head through the gap. "Now you see him," he said. "Now you don't."

Ty turned to Charlie. "That was great, Hitch," he said. "See? I knew you'd help out." He glanced at the elevator operator, who was watching them carefully. "Uh, take us up to Mr. M.'s floor, Brack."

"Of course, Master Yu," Brack said.

The two boys stepped inside the elevator, now back to normal, and watched as the doors slid shut.

The Missing Magician

As Ty led him toward a dim hallway on the fourteenth floor, Charlie turned to wave at Brack.

The elevator door in the middle of the elevator bank was already closing.

That's weird, thought Charlie. *Downstairs, Brack's elevator is on the left. But up here, Brack's door is in the middle of the row of elevators.*

"Hey, Ty," said Charlie, "did you know that —?"

"Yeah, yeah," said Ty, without bothering to stop. "The elevator moves sideways. Don't ask me how. It's magic."

"Yeah, no big deal, just some magic," Charlie muttered, shaking his head. "Okay. Whatever."

They kept walking down the long hall, passing several hallways that branched off to the sides, leading into darkness.

Charlie tried to listen for people inside the rooms, but he didn't hear anything. Not music playing, not a TV, not a voice. Not a breath.

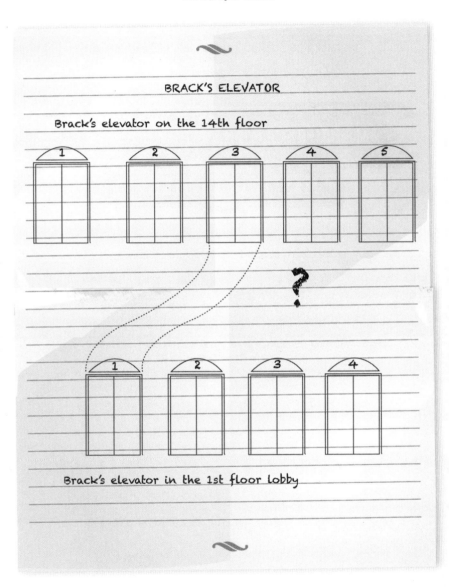

"Here's his room," said Ty, stopping at a door numbered 1413. A sign on the door read:

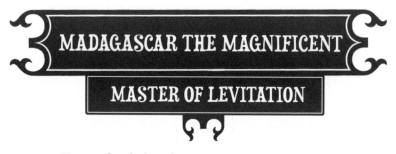

MADAGASCAR THE MAGNIFICENT

MASTER OF LEVITATION

Ty pushed the door open. "It's not locked," he said. "It wasn't yesterday, either."

They stepped inside the apartment of the missing magician. Two figures rushed toward them.

"Look out!" shouted Charlie. "Someone's here!"

Ty snorted. "It's a mirror," he said, rolling his eyes. "And, wow, I figured that out all by myself. I must have acute visual memory."

Charlie ignored him and started walking through the apartment.

A front hallway led to a sitting room, a bedroom, a small kitchen, and a bathroom in the back. Most of the walls were covered with old posters from the days when Madagascar performed around the world.

Ty pointed out various objects as they walked through the rooms. "There's his suitcases, all his shoes, even his wallet," he said. "No one leaves their home without their wallet."

Charlie nodded. He saw a bunch of keys lying on a nearby table. "Are those keys his, too?" he asked.

"Yup," said Ty. "See what I mean? He just vanished. I kept checking this place out all last night, but he never showed up."

"Why would someone leave without their keys?" Charlie said.

"Beats me," said Ty, scratching his neck.

Charlie walked back through the rest of the apartment. Although small, it was very neat. Everything was in its place. Mr. Madagascar's rooms looked like the home of a very organized person.

In the front entry room, Ty stepped on something by the hall table. He bent down and picked up three plastic cylinders. "What do you suppose these are?" he asked.

Charlie looked closely. He stuck his finger through them. Three empty tubes, about the size of his biggest finger. Were they toys? Packages for candy?

I've seen these before, he thought. He was sure of that. But where?

Charlie held the tubes close to his glasses. "They're dated," said Charlie. "From last week. A week ago today, in fact."

"Let me see," said Ty.

Charlie handed them over, and then noticed something on the hall table. A manila folder like the ones his teachers used at school. The folder was marked COME BACK. He felt a little guilty about reading someone else's private papers, but Charlie opened it up and began searching for clues.

Staring at the plastic tubes, Ty said, "Maybe the old guy likes candy." He gave them back to Charlie and then, suddenly, his expression changed. "It's my fault I missed him. I should have come up here when my mom told me. Now I won't get my money this month."

Ty pounded the wall with his fist.

No money. No Tezuki Slamhammer 750.

Charlie was sure that would be the end of his partnership with Ty. Surely the bully would demolish him now.

Suddenly, the lights flickered off and on.

"Not again," Ty groaned.

The lights went out, this time for several seconds. "This is not good," said Ty.

When the lights came back on, Charlie was staring at the mirror. Another face was staring back at him.

An old man's face with bulging eyes and an open mouth. The man's head had poked through the open door behind them.

"That's him!" yelled Ty. "That's Mr. Madagascar!"

Then the man's face disappeared.

The Open Window

The two boys darted out the door.

"Where'd he go?" shouted Charlie.

"This way!" yelled Ty.

Charlie followed Ty through a maze of long, endless corridors.

The sound of footsteps ahead of them was their only guide. Then the footsteps stopped.

"Did we lose him?" asked Charlie.

"I don't know," Ty said.

A cold October breeze passed down the hall. Somewhere, a window was open. Without warning, Ty shouted angrily and banged his fist against a wall. "What an idiot!" he muttered.

Then a door nearby creaked open. A woman's voice called out, "What's all this ruckus? What's going on?"

The two boys followed the voice and turned a corner. An older woman stood there, leaning against a doorframe. Light spilled from her room and glittered on the fancy red bathrobe wrapped tightly around her.

"Is that you, Tyler?" she said. Charlie noticed that the woman's cheeks were bright pink.

"Sorry, Miss Drake," replied Ty. "We've been chasing someone."

"Chasing someone?" she cried. "Heavens to Betsy! I thought the hotel was falling down, with all that noise."

Ty introduced Charlie to the woman. Dotty Drake had once worked with magic herself. She had been a magician's assistant. "One of the best," she said, smiling.

"Were you sawn in half, or did you float through the air?" Charlie asked.

"A little of both," said Miss Drake.

"Sorry to butt in, Miss D., but did you hear anyone else run past your apartment tonight?" asked Ty.

"I heard lots of running," said the woman. "But who would be running around here?" She stopped. She raised a hand to her mouth.

The lights flickered off and on again.

"Him . . ." she said faintly. With her other hand she pointed back down the hallway, behind the boys.

Charlie turned and saw a shadowy figure standing near the middle of the hall.

"Mr. Madagascar," called Ty. "Is that you?"

The figure shouted back. "I'm sorry, young man. But I have to do this."

"What's going on?" said Miss Drake.

The lights flickered off and on. Miss Drake screamed and fell to the floor. "Oh no!" yelled Charlie. He and Ty knelt down beside her.

The lights turned off for several more seconds.

When they came back on, the older woman's eyes fluttered.

"You must stop him," she said.

The boys looked back down the hall. The shadowy man was now standing at the far end, next to an open window. A breeze was blowing the purple curtains that hung on either side of the window.

"Wait!" cried Ty. "Mr. M.! What are you doing?"

Then, as Charlie watched, not believing his eyes, the man called Mr. Madagascar took a running start and leaped headfirst through the open window into the darkness beyond.

The Master of Levitation

Miss Drake screamed again.

Ty jumped up and hurried down the long hallway. Just as he passed another hall, a second shadowy figure appeared.

It collided with Ty. A shudder passed through the hall. Then Ty groaned and collapsed, and the lights continued to flicker off and on.

At the far end, the window still stood open. The curtains rustled in the night wind. The sound of cars and traffic floated up from the streets below.

Charlie ran to the middle of the hall. "Ty, are you okay?" he asked.

In the darkness, Ty mumbled, "Where is he?"

The lights turned back on. Charlie ran over to the open window. He brushed aside the waving curtains and leaned out.

Far below on the sidewalk, people walked along as if nothing had happened.

The outside of the building was smooth. The nearest windows were closed.

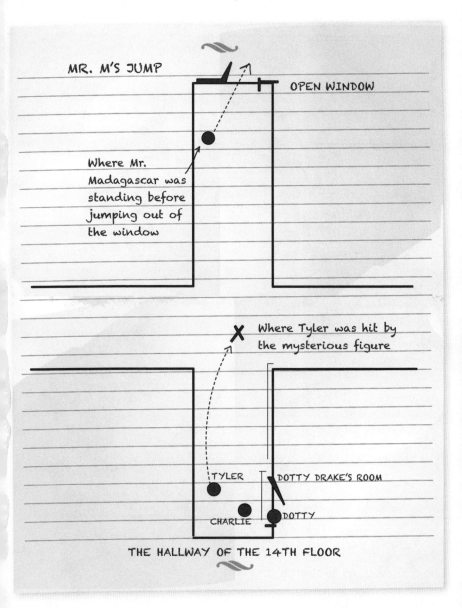

MR. M'S JUMP

OPEN WINDOW

Where Mr. Madagascar was standing before jumping out of the window

Where Tyler was hit by the mysterious figure

TYLER

DOTTY DRAKE'S ROOM

CHARLIE

DOTTY

THE HALLWAY OF THE 14TH FLOOR

It was a straight shot down, at least a dozen stories to the ground. There was no ledge, no roof, no awning, nothing that would have slowed down, or caught the body of the falling Mr. Madagascar. Where was he?

Miss Drake joined Charlie at the open window and looked out cautiously. The breeze tugged at her silver hair.

"What happened?" she asked. "Where is he?"

"Gone," said Charlie.

Miss Drake's face turned pale. Charlie was afraid she was going to faint again.

"That's impossible, young man," she said.

"Even for a magician?" asked Charlie.

The older woman stared hard at him. There was a glint of steel in her eyes.

"Maybe not," she said. She looked at the sidewalk far below. Then her gaze wandered to the buildings across the street. "He was the Master of Levitation, after all," she said.

"But that's just fake magic," said Charlie. "I mean, it was a trick, right?"

"A trick?" asked Miss Drake, leaning out the window for a final look. "Well, if it was a trick, then it was the greatest magic trick in the world. Madagascar would be the first human to fly!"

That's impossible, Charlie thought. But a little voice inside him added, *Or is it?*

Miss Drake adjusted her red robe, and Charlie noticed that it matched the waving curtains behind her. *That's funny,* thought Charlie. *I thought the drapes were purple.*

Miss Drake said, "We need to take Tyler downstairs."

Ty was sitting on the carpet, holding his head in his hands. "Where is he?" he mumbled again.

"Mr. Madagascar jumped out the window," said Charlie. "Um, do you think you might have a concussion?"

Ty shook his head. "No, I mean the guy who ran into me."

In the craziness, Charlie had forgotten all about that second figure. The lights had been going off and on then. The shadowy stranger must have escaped during a blackout.

"I didn't get a good look at him," said Ty. "He looked tough, though."

"I didn't see him either," said Charlie. He looked closer at Ty and added, "You look terrible." Ty's face was covered in bruises. "You two really banged into each other."

"That should make him easy to find," said Ty, slowly getting to his feet. "Keep your eyes open for some jerk who looks like me, covered in bruises."

"Let's get you downstairs," said Miss Drake.

They took an elevator to the first floor and led Ty to his family's rooms behind the lobby.

Mrs. Yu was upset when they walked in. "Tyler! I've been looking everywhere for you," she cried.

As soon as she gave her son a closer look, she screamed. "Look at your face!" she yelled. "What happened to you? Go wash that off in the bathroom. And who is your friend?"

"This is just a kid from school," Ty said. "And I'm okay," he added.

"Does this have to do with Mr. Madagascar?" Mrs. Yu asked.

"Um, sort of," Ty said. "He jumped out the window."

Mrs. Yu shrieked. "I'm calling the police!" she said. "These crazy magicians —!"

Ty hurried Charlie down the hall as Mrs. Yu ran into the kitchen.

In the bathroom, Charlie helped Ty wash crusted blood off his forehead. "I do look terrible," said Ty, staring into the mirror.

"You look like you ran into a wall," said Charlie. "A couple of walls."

Ty snorted. "Well, man, it's all over. I can't get money from a guy who jumped out a window."

Charlie looked at Ty's reflection in the mirror. "I'm not so sure of that," he said.

"Are you kidding?" said Ty. He balled a towel up tightly in his fist. "Madagascar jumped out that window. We both saw him."

"We need to go back upstairs," said Charlie. "Before the police get here. We need to examine the scene of the crime. And," he added, "we need to figure out what these are." He pulled the strange plastic tubes from Mr. Madagascar's apartment out of his pocket.

"And figure out what those dates on them mean," said Ty.

"The dates are from one week ago today," said Charlie. "And didn't you say the lights were blinking off and on last week, too?"

Ty nodded thoughtfully. "Hey, have you noticed that the lights aren't blinking anymore?" he said.

Good call, thought Charlie.

In fact, the lights had stopped flickering ever since Mr. Madagascar jumped. Was the blinking light somehow connected with the magician's disappearance?

"Okay, let's go back," said Tyler, throwing down the towel. "Come on."

Clues and Cents

Tyler and Charlie ran down a hall behind the Yus' apartment.

"There's a way back to the elevators around here," called Ty.

When they got to the elevator bank, Mr. Brack's car was open. The boys rushed inside.

"The fourteenth floor?" asked the operator. Charlie was silent. He was busy thinking of all the clues in this puzzle.

"Hey, Hitch," said Ty. "We're going back to Mr. M's, right?"

The old elevator operator leaned toward Charlie and grinned. "A penny for your thoughts, Master Hitchcock."

Penny? thought Charlie. *Yes, pennies made sense!*

"Wait!" he said. "All the stuff I've seen tonight. It's all smooshed together like a jigsaw puzzle. You know that the teachers said I had a —"

"Yeah, yeah," said Ty. "A photographic memory."

"Exactly," Charlie said. "So here's what we definitely know." He listed all the clues they'd come across that night.

TONIGHT'S CLUES

1. The plastic tubes in Mr. M's room

2. The folder on his table

3. Brack's vanishing trick in the elevator

4. Brack saying that the hotel had (magic)? in its walls

5. The blackouts one week ago
   ↳ suspicious

6. The color of the drapes of the window Mr. M. jumped out of. Red? Purple?

7. The color of Miss Drake's robe, and Miss Drake's scream

8. The neon sign of the rabbit and the hat outside the hotel

"The color of the drapes was purple," said Ty. "At least I think that's what I saw before I got knocked down. Let's go back up and check."

"Not yet," said Charlie. "We need to go to the basement."

Mr. Brack kept grinning, and down the elevator zoomed. At the bottom, the boys found themselves in the huge cellar and power center of the hotel.

"Where are the fuses?" asked Charlie.

Ty led him to a small room at the back of the cellar. The walls of the room were lined with old metal boxes. The boxes all hung about four feet above the damp floor. It reminded Charlie of a miniature locker room. On the closed doors of the metal boxes were labels: First Floor, Second Floor, and so on.

e use them at
out of change,"

rlie. "Anyway,
causing those

sked.

isn't any
"That's
pennies. In
ought last
te stamped on
someone was
out."

vere for candy
id Ty. "So how
thing?"

es before, but
id Charlie.

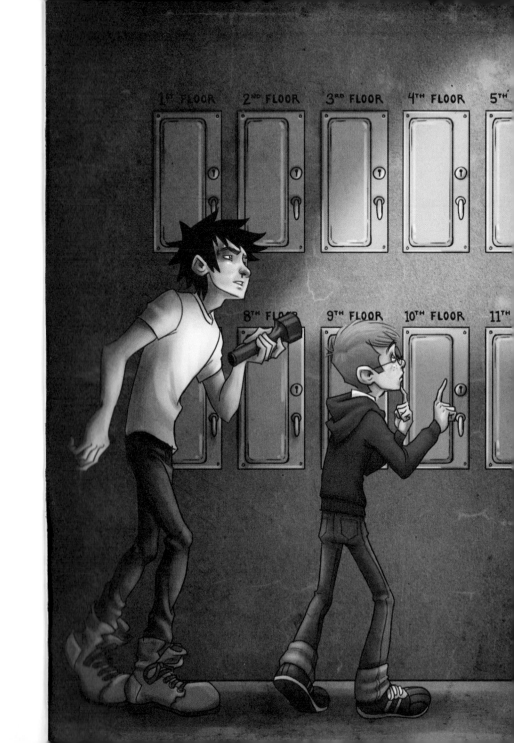

"Nice. I thought they'd have the old or down here," said Charlie. "We need to fin the fuse box for the fourteenth floor."

After a few minutes of searching, and reading faded numbers on the boxes, Ty found the right one.

"Here it is," he said, nodding. "Fourteenth floor."

"Did you have to come down here last week to check on things? When the power went out?" asked Charlie.

"No, the problem didn't last that long," Ty said. "It came back on by itself. We thought maybe it was the thunderstorm th night."

Charlie carefully opened the fuse box. Dust covered everything . . . except for son small circular shapes on the bottom lip of the box.

"Oh yeah. I've seen peop cash registers when they run said Ty.

"Right, exactly," said Ch this proves that someone wa blackouts on purpose."

"How do you know?" Ty

"These circles where there dust?" Charlie said, pointing where someone put a stack c fact, since the pennies were I week — the tubes had the do them, remember? — it mean planning for the lights going

"Ha! And I thought they and he had a sweet tooth," s did you figure out the penny

"I'd seen those plastic tub couldn't remember where," s

"How'd you remember?" Ty asked.

"When Brack said 'A penny for your thoughts,'" Charlie said. "That's when it all came together."

"Huh. Pretty smart, Hitch," said Ty.

Brack doesn't miss much, thought Charlie. *It's almost like he knows everything that's going on in the hotel. But now we need to go —*

"I think we need to go back to the fourteenth floor," said Ty.

"You read my mind," said Charlie.

Magic in the Walls

Tyler and Charlie knocked on Dottie Drake's apartment door. They heard noises behind the door and then a voice. "It's very late. Who is it?"

"It's me again," said Ty. "Tyler Yu. Sorry to bother you, but it's very important."

The door opened slowly. Dottie Drake stood there, wrapped in her red robe. "I was asleep," she said, yawning, patting her pile of hair.

Charlie noticed that the woman's cheeks were still pink. "Are you wearing makeup, Miss Drake?" he asked.

Miss Drake's eyes grew wide. "What on earth are you —?"

"You said you were asleep, but you're wearing makeup," Charlie said. "Just like you were when we first saw you."

"Artists always wear makeup," she said.

"When they sleep?" said Charlie. "I think you were wearing makeup because you were expecting company. And you weren't sleeping just now, either."

"Tyler, your friend is an insulting little boor," said Miss Drake.

"And I think you know what happened to Mr. Madagascar," said Charlie.

"I am going back to bed!" said Miss Drake. She tried to shut the door, but Charlie stopped her.

"The police are coming," said Charlie. "The Yus are calling them. Don't you want to hear what I have to say before they get here?"

"I don't know what you're talking about," Miss Drake said.

"Just come over to the window," said Charlie.

The three of them walked down the hall to the window where Mr. Madagascar had jumped.

Charlie raised his eyebrow at Ty.

"Yeah, I see it now," said Ty. "The drapes are red. They match the color of Miss Drake's bathrobe."

"So?" Miss Drake said.

"That's right," said Charlie. "When you and I came over to the window and saw that Mr. M. had vanished, I saw that your gown matched the drapes. Red. In fact, if you look, all the drapes in the hall windows are red. But when Mr. M. jumped out the window, they were purple."

"You must be mistaken," said Miss Drake.

"No, I saw it too," said Ty.

"So then I wondered how red drapes could turn purple," said Charlie.

He walked back down the hall toward the intersection where Ty had been hit. Then Charlie turned to his left and walked down that side hall. He stopped at the end, next to its window.

"Look at these," said Charlie. Ty ran up to him. Miss Drake slowly followed.

"Purple!" said Ty. "But how?"

The boys leaned out the window. To the right, they saw the blue neon sign of the rabbit and the magician's hat.

"Blue and red make purple," said Charlie. "That's how."

"And look down there," said Ty.

A few feet below the window was a wide ledge that ran along that side of the hotel. "If someone jumped out *this* window, they'd land on that ledge."

"But we all thought he jumped out the other window," said Charlie. "Where there was a straight drop to the street."

"It was an amazing magic trick," said Dottie Drake.

"Yes, it was," said Charlie. "But not a trick of levitation, or floating. It was a trick with mirrors."

"Just like Brack's trick in the elevator," said Ty, nodding.

"Brack said the hotel's walls were full of magic," said Charlie. "And I believe it. If a magician built this place, why wouldn't he put in all kinds of tricks and illusions, for the fun of the guests?"

"How come I didn't know about them?" Ty asked.

Charlie shrugged. "Over all the years, I'm sure many of them were forgotten. But Mr. M. is a magician himself. He'd know what to look for."

Charlie led them back to the intersection of the two hallways. He carefully examined one of the corners. "Look!" he said triumphantly. "This pulls out!" He gripped a small handle hidden in the wooden molding of the corner's edge. Out came a panel as tall as the wall itself. Smoothly, it glided over to the opposite corner, forming an angle in the hallway. The secret panel was a single, huge mirror.

"Another magic trick," said Ty.

From where the two boys had stood at Miss Drake's apartment, it looked as if they were staring straight down the hall.

But instead, the mirror was reflecting the side hall, the real hallway that Mr. Madagascar had run down. He had thrown himself out the side window and safely landed on the ledge. But the mirror had tricked his small audience into believing he had jumped out the other window and disappeared.

"It's still a good trick," said Dottie Drake, sadly.

"A magnificent trick!" boomed a voice behind them.

Mr. Madagascar stepped out from Miss Drake's apartment. "And no one else had thought of it," he said.

He walked up to Ty and Charlie. "A man jumps out a window and disappears fourteen floors above the ground. Good one, huh?" said the magician.

"Yes," said Charlie. "But why?"

"This was supposed to be the beginning of my comeback," Mr. Madagascar said. "I wanted to perform one last show, one astounding trick that would go down in the history books."

"So you planned all of this?" asked Ty.

"Of course I did," said Mr. Madagascar. "I waited for you to come up to my apartment, and I wanted you to follow me. I had everything all set up. And the lovely Miss Drake here helped by providing some misdirection." He winked at Dottie, who blushed.

Right. Misdirection like Brack performed earlier, thought Charlie. *When he pointed toward the lobby and said, "Now you see him, now you don't." He made us turn around so he could close the two fake mirror walls in the elevator.*

"So Miss Drake's scream was the misdirection," said Ty.

"I always had a good voice for that," Miss Drake said proudly, putting her hand to her throat. "And while I screamed and fainted, the mirror wall slid back into the corner."

"It's on a timer," Mr. Madagascar explained.

Ty laughed. "So the guy who knocked me down was me!" he said. "My own reflection." He flexed his muscles and added, "I knew he looked tough."

A low hum rumbled in the hall. The mirror glided back into the corner and snapped into place. And outside the building, a siren wailed.

"I didn't break any law," said Mr. Madagascar.

"But the police will want to know what happened," said Ty.

"Do they have to know tonight?" asked the magician. "Give me twenty-four hours. Give me time to have the headlines proclaim my trick to the world. Then I will reappear, and make a statement to the press."

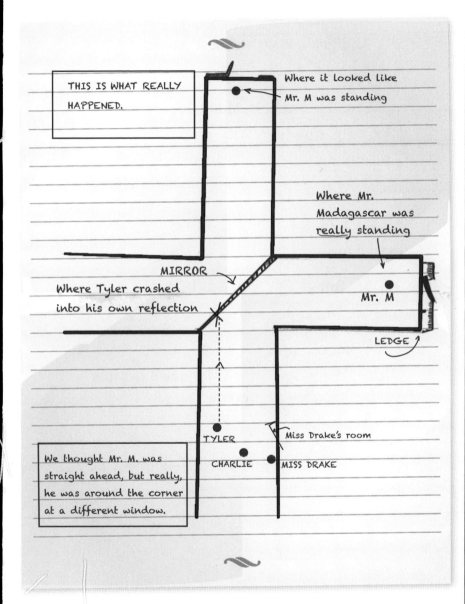

THIS IS WHAT REALLY HAPPENED.

Where it looked like Mr. M was standing

Where Mr. Madagascar was really standing

MIRROR

Where Tyler crashed into his own reflection

Mr. M

LEDGE

TYLER

Miss Drake's room

CHARLIE

MISS DRAKE

We thought Mr. M. was straight ahead, but really, he was around the corner at a different window.

"And you'll have the best publicity in the world," said Charlie, smiling.

"Exactly," said Mr. Madagascar. "Publicity. And then I can plan my final performance and end with the window trick."

The magician and the former assistant looked at the boys.

"My fate — our fate — is in your hands," said Mr. Madagascar.

Ty glanced over at Charlie, and then back at the magician. "As long as I get this month's rent," Ty said.

"Deal!" exclaimed Mr. Madagascar. "Now come to my room and I will give you your cash."

Ty pumped his fist in the air. "Yeah," he said. "Slamhammer!"

Mr. Madagascar looked confused, but he put his fist in the air too. "Indeed, Slamhammer!" he said.

More Secrets

The next morning proved Mr. Madagascar and Miss Drake right. Newspapers, TV stations, and online channels were full of the mysterious disappearance of the magician from the Abracadabra Hotel's fourteenth floor.

Everyone was talking about it, trying to solve the puzzle. There was even a new website — How Did He Do It? — where people posted their own solutions to the mystery.

True to his word, Mr. Madagascar reappeared at the hotel later that day. He gave a press conference that afternoon, and explained that he would soon perform the trick before the eyes of the public, in one last final show of magic.

Of course, everyone at Blackstone Middle School was talking about it. But they were more interested in an even more amazing event.

That morning, when Tyler Yu and Charlie Hitchcock returned to school, it was Tyler who was covered with bruises and cuts.

Charlie seemed perfectly fine.

"Unbelievable," said Charlie's best friend, Andrew, as they sat down to lunch, everyone in the cafeteria staring at Charlie. "You are the only person to beat up Tyler Yu!"

Charlie looked up from his lunch. "Who said I beat him up?"

"But just look at him," said Andrew. "You obviously won the fight."

"Don't always trust what you can see," said Charlie.

* * *

That day, two secret notes changed hands. In the break between English and American History, Charlie and Ty each shoved a note in the other's hand. No one saw.

Ty read his note in his seat at the back of the classroom.

I solved the puzzle of the moving elevator.

Brack's elevator on the 14th floor (#3)

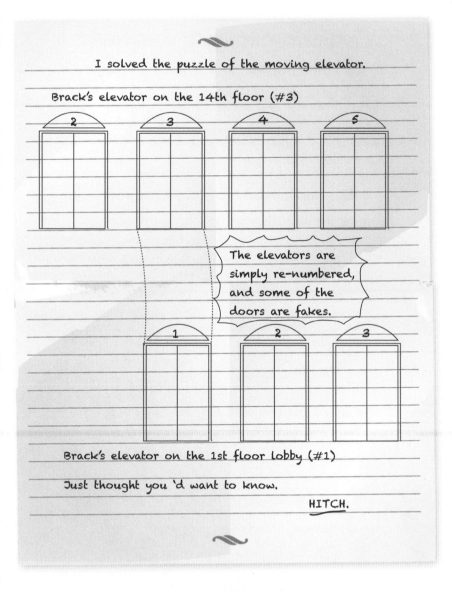

The elevators are simply re-numbered, and some of the doors are fakes.

Brack's elevator on the 1st floor lobby (#1)

Just thought you'd want to know.

HITCH.

At his own desk, Charlie unfolded his note.

DON'T TELL ANYONE ABOUT ME RUNNING INTO THE MIRROR. OR ELSE.

I WONDER IF YOU'RE SMART ENOUGH TO HELP ME WITH ANOTHER SMALL PROBLEM.

I THINK THE HOTEL HAS A GHOST.

ABOUT THE AUTHOR

MICHAEL DAHL grew up reading everything he could find about his hero Harry Houdini, and worked as a magician's assistant when he was a teenager. Even though he cannot disappear, he is very good at escaping things. Dahl has written the popular Library of Doom series, the Dragonblood books, and the Finnegan Zwake series. He currently lives in the Midwest in a haunted house.

ABOUT THE ILLUSTRATOR

LISA K. WEBER is an illustrator currently living in Oakland, California. She graduated from Parsons School of Design in 2000 and then began freelancing. Since then, she has completed many print, animation, and design projects, including graphic novelizations of classic literature, character and background designs for children's cartoons, and textiles for dog clothing.

DISCUSSION QUESTIONS

1. At the beginning of the book, Charlie thought Ty was a bully. What do you think? Is Ty a bully? Explain your answer.

2. Have you seen a magic show? Talk about some of the tricks you saw.

3. Would you want to stay at the Abracadabra Hotel? Why or why not?

WRITING PROMPTS

1. Imagine that Ty had chosen you to help him solve the mystery at the hotel. Write a short story from your point of view. How could you have helped him?

2. Create your own magic trick. What is it? How does it work?

3. Pretend that you're traveling and you stay at the Abracadabra Hotel. Write a letter to a friend talking about your vacation.

GLOSSARY

acute (uh-KYOOT)—sharp

collided (kuh-LIDE-id)—crashed forcefully

concussion (kun-KUSH-uhn)—an injury to the brain caused by a heavy blow to the head

curious (KYUR-ee-uhss)—eager to find out

interior (in-TEER-ee-ur)—the inside of something

misdirection (miss-der-EKT-shuhn)—sending someone the wrong way, or shifting someone's attention to something else

photographic (foh-toe-GRAF-ik)—like taking pictures

publicity (puh-BLISS-uh-tee)—information about a person or event that is given out to get the public's attention or approval

reasoning (REE-zuhn-ing)—process of thinking in an orderly fashion

retired (ri-TIRED)—gave up work

temper (TEM-pur)—a tendency to get angry

visual (VIZH-oo-uhl)—to do with seeing

THE ESCAPING COIN

Big or small, all magic tricks are just illusions. Sometimes the best illusions are when the magic happens right in a person's hand. This one will leave the whole audience baffled!

You need: Seven Pennies

PERFORMANCE:

1. First, tell the audience that money sometimes has a mind of its own and likes to escape. Pick up the pennies one at a time and place them in your left hand. Count them out loud so the audience knows how many there are.

2. Now ask a volunteer to hold out his or her hand. Count out loud as you transfer the coins, one at a time, from your hand into the volunteer's hand.

3. When you get to the sixth penny, tap it against the coins in the volunteer's hand as shown. The sound will cause the volunteer and the audience to believe that it landed with the other coins.

4. Instead of giving the volunteer the sixth penny, simply keep it hidden in your right hand. This will take practice so the volunteer doesn't see that you keep it. Now drop the last penny into the volunteer's hand as shown. Ask your volunteer to close his or her hand tightly so no coins can escape.

Hidden coin

5. Put your hand hiding the secret penny under the volunteer's hand in a fist as shown. Bump the volunteer's hand a couple of times, then let the hidden coin drop into your left hand as shown. Finally, ask the volunteer to count out the number of coins he or she has in their hand. When the volunteer counts only six coins, the audience will think the coin escaped right through your volunteer's closed hand!

Like this trick? Learn more in the book *Amazing Magic Tricks: Expert Level* by Norm Barnhart!
All images and text © 2009 Capstone Press. Used by permission.